What Dads Can't Do

by
Douglas Wood

pictures by
Doug Cushman

Simon & Schuster Books for Young Readers
New York   London   Toronto   Sydney

There are lots of things
that regular people can do
but dads can't.

Dads can't cross the street
without holding hands.

Dads can push,
  but they can't swing.

Dads can't pitch a baseball very hard

or hit one very far.

Dads aren't good at sleeping late.

They can't comb their hair

or shave by themselves.

Dads like to go camping,
    but they need lots of help
    setting up the tent.

And cooking.

Dads like to go fishing,
    but they don't like to go alone.

And they need extra practice baiting the hook.

Dads seem to have trouble holding on to their money.

Dads can't see you hiding your lima beans
at dinnertime.
Or feeding them to the cat.

Dads like to give baths,
but they can't help
getting all wet.

Sometimes they leave a night-light on
    because they're a little bit scared of the dark.
They also like to check under the bed for monsters.

There are so many things that dads can't do
        it's a wonder they make it through life
        at all.
But dads can't give up.
No matter how tired a dad gets,
        or how hard life gets,
        a dad never quits.

And most of all,
    whatever happens,
    a dad never ever stops
    loving you.